THE BLUE POOL
OF QUESTIONS

By Maya Abu-Alhayyat
Illustrated by Hassan Manasrah
Translated by Hanan Awad

penny
candy
BOOKS

Penny Candy Books
Oklahoma City & Savannah
Translation © 2017 Penny Candy Books

Originally published as *Berkat Al Asela Al Zarqa'a* © Palestine Writing
Workshop, 2016.

 This book is printed on paper certified to the environmental and social
FSC standards of the Forest Stewardship Council™ (FSC®).

Design: Shanna Compton, shannacompton.com

Photo of Maya Abu-Alhayyat by Salim Abu Jabal
Photo of Hassan Manasrah by Momin Bannani
Photo of Hanan Awad by Hamzah Saadah

Thanks to Mohammad Alshaibani for the coffeeshop conversation during the
making of this translation.

21 20 19 18 17   1 2 3 4 5
ISBN-13: 978-0-9972219-8-5 (paperback)
ISBN-13: 978-0-9987999-0-2 (hardcover)

Books for the kid in *all* of us
www.pennycandybooks.com

Some time ago,
an odd man traveled the
city streets alone.

He was often happy and
kind, though sometimes
he seemed sad and scary.

But he was always alone.

He sang strange tunes.
Dried flowers fell from his sleeves.
Books slept inside his coat like shoes in a closet.

From the flowers, he created a festival of colors for the people of the city while he warbled his old, annoying songs.

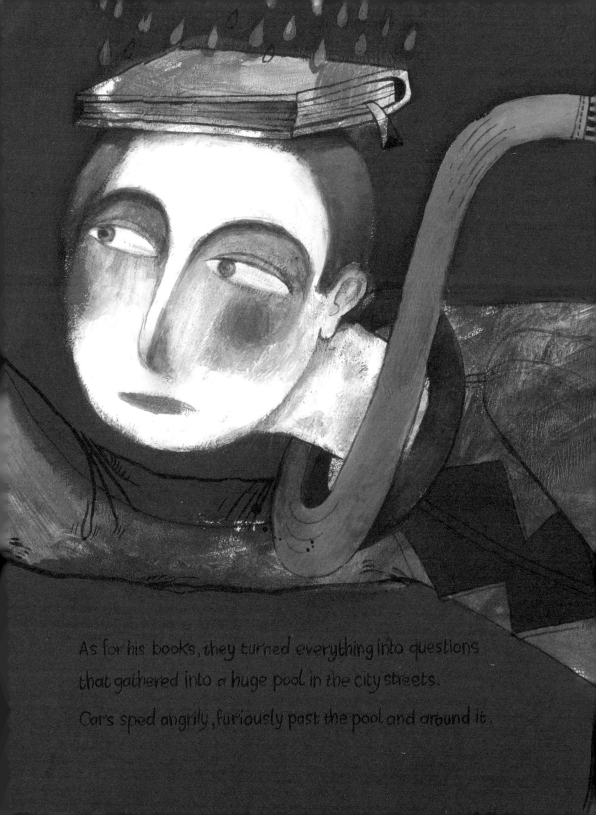

As for his books, they turned everything into questions
that gathered into a huge pool in the city streets.

Cars sped angrily, furiously past the pool and around it.

By winter, the pool looked like a lake, then an ocean.
Everyone complained. No one wanted to swim across,
but they all had somewhere to go: to school, home, work,
where they had answers to their questions. They knew everyday answers
so well that they had forgotten what questions looked like,
and the pool of questions frightened them.

When spring arrived,

the man waited with everyone else.

He had always done a lot of waiting.

By summer, he decided to dive
into the pool. He tried,
but at first he couldn't.   All those questions!

The pool seemed deep and scary, even to him.
He did not enjoy swimming alone.

The man looked into the pool.
Gazing deep and far,
he saw something shining
and heard a voice that said,

"Come in.
I am the Answer."

The Answer gave its hand to the man and said again, "Come in."

A car honked its horn behind them. The entire city urged him, "Go."

They were tired of the man and his pool of questions.

So the man put on his yellow shorts and leaped into the pool.

He swam to a place where there was no summer or winter,

no spring or fall. Where there were no questions and no answers.

Where everything outside the pool seemed small.

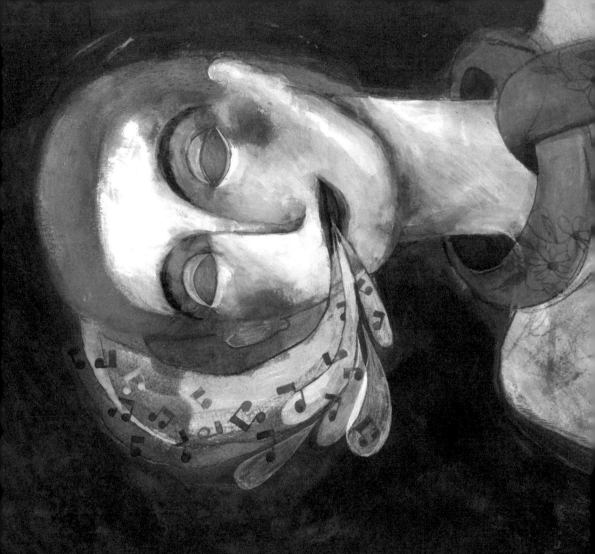

In that place, no one asked him, "Why do you walk alone?"

"Why are you so strange?"

"Why do dried flowers fall from your sleeves?"

"Why do old, annoying songs fall from your Lips?"

Sitting down, the man pulled a yellow flower

and a bundle of green onions from his sleeve.

He ate the onions and fed the sleepy stars, too.

The Answer sat next to the man and told him about how

it had been stuck in the pool for ages, unable to get out.

The man and the Answer became friends.
Both had been alone for a long time.
Both were kind.
Neither of them, not even the Answer,
knew anything but questions.

With the threads of their conversation,
the man sewed a curtain,
fastening it to the sky
to protect him from the jeers
and scowls of the people.

Nowadays, if the stars look like a lonely man eating onions and snoring, or like a man who wraps himself in all the answers, he's just reminding us to ask more questions, throw them into the blue pool, be brave, and dive in.

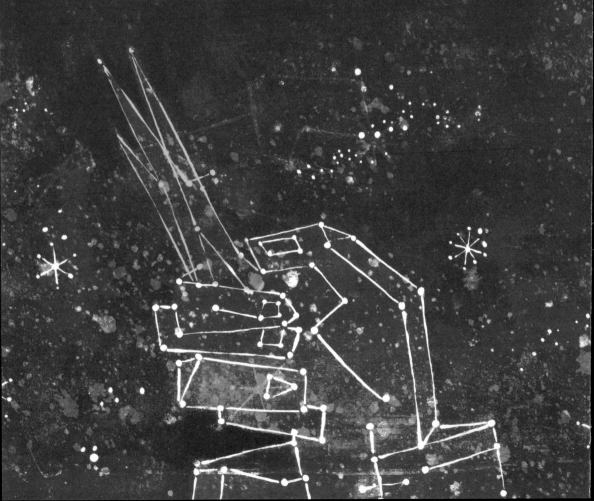

MAYA ABU-ALHAYYAT is an award-winning Palestinian novelist, poet, and children's book writer. She has published three collections of poetry: *Home Dresses and Wars* (Dar Alahlyah, 2016), *This Smile, That Heart* (Dar Raya, 2012), *What She Said about Him* (House of Poetry & Qattan Foundation, 2007); three novels: *Bloodtype* (Dar el-Adab, 2013), *Grains of Sugar* (House of Poetry, 2004), *Threshold of Heavy Spirit* (Ogarit, 2011); and several children's books. Her writing has been featured in international journals and magazines and has been translated into English, French, German, Swedish, and Korean. Since 2013 Maya has worked as the director of the Palestinian Writing Workshop in Birzeit. She currently lives in Jerusalem with her husband and children.

HASSAN MANASRAH is a visual artist, illustrator, and comic creator. He studied interior design at al Balqa Applied University and painting at the Jordanian Fine Art Center. He also studied printmaking at the Jordanian Fine Art Museum where he concentrated on lithography, etching zinc and copper, and lino- and monoprints. From 2008 to 2010, he worked as assistant art director for the animated cartoon series *Pink Panther & Pals*. Since 2010, he has illustrated 25 children books. In 2014, the book *Why Not?*, illustrated by Manasrah, was shortlisted for the Etisalat Award for Arabic Children's Literature for best illustration and made the White Ravens list. In 2016, he won an Etisalat Award for best illustration for the Palestinian edition of *The Blue Pool of Questions*.

HANAN AWAD, known to most as Debwania, is a Palestinian-American living in Edmond, Oklahoma, USA. Debwania is an established street photographer selected by well-known Palestinian journalist photographer Osama Silwadi to be a member of the Arab Photo Agency. She received her undergraduate degree in Middle Eastern Studies from Rutgers University, a filmmaking certificate from New York Film Academy, where she also studied photography, and is currently completing her Masters in History at University of Central Oklahoma with a focus on Latin America and the Middle East.